W9-CSS-610

♫...with a little help from my friends.♫

For Geoff, Sue, Abby, Hannah, Nick & Polly, with love.

Text and illustrations copyright © 1986 by Jill Murphy.
All rights reserved. G. P. Putnam's Sons, 200 Madison Avenue, NYC 10016.

Originated and published in Great Britain by Walker Books Ltd., 1986.
Printed in Hong Kong by Imago.
L.C. Number: 86–643.
First American edition, 1986.
ISBN 0-399-21354-6 (hardcover edition)
5 7 9 10 8 6
First American miniature edition, 1989.
ISBN 0-399-21938-2 (miniature edition)
3 5 7 9 10 8 6 4 2

Five Minutes' Peace

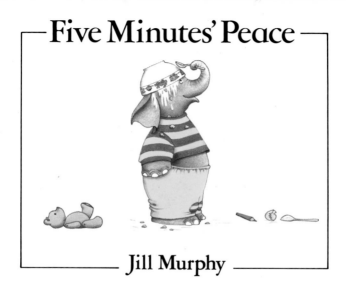

Jill Murphy

G.P. Putnam's Sons   New York

The children were having breakfast.
This was not a pleasant sight.

Mrs. Large took a tray from the cupboard. She set it with a teapot, a milk jug, her favorite cup and saucer, a plate of marmalade toast and a leftover cake from yesterday. She stuffed the morning paper into her pocket and sneaked off toward the door.

"Where are you going with that tray, Mom?" asked Laura.

"To the bathroom," said Mrs. Large.

"Why?" asked the other two children.

"Because I want five minutes' peace from all of *you*," said Mrs. Large. "That's why."

"Can *we* come?" asked Lester as they trailed
  up the stairs behind her.
"No," said Mrs. Large, "you can't."
"What shall *we* do then?" asked Laura.
"You can play," said Mrs. Large. "Downstairs.
  By yourselves. And keep an eye on the baby."
"I'm *not* a baby," muttered the little one.

Mrs. Large ran a deep, hot bath.
She emptied half a bottle of bubble bath
into the water, plunked on her shower cap
and got in. She poured herself a cup of tea
and lay back with her eyes closed.
It was heaven.

"Can I play you my tune?" asked Lester.

Mrs. Large opened one eye. "Must you?" she asked.

"I've been practicing," said Lester. "You told me to. *Can* I? Please, just for *one* minute."

"Go *on*, then," sighed Mrs. Large.

So Lester played. He played "Twinkle, Twinkle, Little Star" three and a half times.

In came Laura. "Can I read you a page from
my reading book?" she asked.

"*No,* Laura," said Mrs. Large. "Go on, *all* of you,
off downstairs."

"You let Lester play his tune," said Laura.

"I heard. You like him better than me. It's not fair."

"Oh, don't be silly, Laura," said Mrs. Large.

"Go *on* then. Just *one* page."

So Laura read. She read four and a half pages
of "Little Red Riding Hood."

In came the little one with a trunkful of toys.
"For *you*!" he beamed, flinging them all
into the bath water.
"Thank you, dear," said Mrs. Large weakly.

"Can I see the cartoons in the paper?" asked Laura.

"Can I have the cake?" asked Lester.

"Can I get in with you?" asked the little one.

Mrs. Large groaned.

In the end they *all* got in. The
little one was in such a hurry that
he forgot to take off his pajamas.

Mrs. Large got out. She dried
herself, put on her bathrobe
and headed for the door.
"Where are you going *now*, Mom?"
asked Laura.
"To the kitchen," said Mrs. Large.
"Why?" asked Lester.
"Because I want five minutes'
peace from all of *you*," said
Mrs. Large. "That's why."

And off she went downstairs, where she had three minutes and forty-five seconds of peace before they all came to join her.